Never say: "I've no idea."

Never say "I'm stuck!"

Reach for these pages and have a read

Be inspired by this book.

CH21-1-66-SSS-Pr

A compendium of Notes, Rhymes and Ideas for stories. Some made it some didn't.

I challenged myself to keep a track of my writing inspiration, beyond the books I am currently creating.

I hope it will entertain, but I do know it's a window into my mind hinting at what will be written.

Nitere Publishing:

ISBN: 978-1-9998113-8-9

Worldwide Copyright ©2021

All rights reserved by the author

Supernatural & Science Sparks

A book to help inspire...
any creator who thinks they are out of ideas.
And...
maybe, people will stop asking me what I write.

A fear, a thought, a joy, remorse,
I've found them all a writer's source.
Without hesitation, I thank my wife
For putting up with my strange life

Follow: @CHart_author

Warning: (Contains Cynicism)

Twitter tags I commonly use to exercise my writing:
#vss365
#writingcommunity

Swan Song

We've weathered the storm for fifty plus
years
With laughter, excitement pathos and tears.
The knurled flaky bark has grown thick in
that time.
I've never written or thought in rhyme.
So, I have to consider these thoughts are not
mine,
The memes think my brain is at the end of
the line.

To Be a Poem...

A poem is a simple thing
Made up when words align
They have a certain cadence
A beat that stays in time.
Though sometimes misconstrued,
The meaning oft sublime,
The key part no-one really gets...

Is it supposed to rhyme?

Zombie Locomotion

"Well, we're here in Graumann's Chinese Theatre... and it's a galaxy of stars on the red carpet."

"...but they're all dead. Look they're walking around like zombies"

"I never understood why the dead walk."

"Have you ever seen one ride a bike?"

"No, but they still have their wallets. Why not pay for a taxi?"

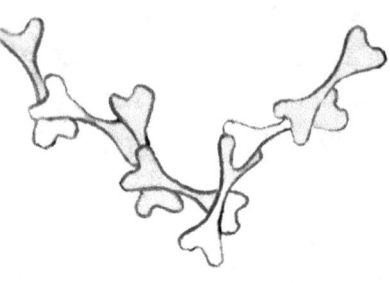

Chthonic Power

Two children were sitting with comics in
hand
Fighting mind battles in air and on land.

A brash young lad, like all young males,
A quiet young girl entranced by dark tales.

"I'd like powers of strength, fire and might!"
"No! Chthonic powers to set darkness alight."

"To squash you or fry you? I'd have to decide."
"You'd lose to an arrow from the dark, where
I'd hide."

"I'd burn up your arrow, snatch it from the
air"
"But your mind would be open and I'd be in
there."

The boy was disturbed and he shuffled away.
She smiled, "Come with me,
there's a game we can play."

A Solar foodie limerick

The Sun roasts Venus and small Mercury
While Jupiter eats meteors mercilessly.
Neptune wants it hot,
While Uranus does not
And Saturn had a Mars before yesterday's tea.

Empathy Force

"We need to keep this between us son." The bullet was close to the heart, his father was dying; he could feel the fear.

"Don't let them know... your gift."

He took his father's pain he added it to his fear and loss and unleashed it against the soldiers.

Empathy was no longer passive.

𝕶night 𝕳orror (Original)

A Medieval Bard's tale.

To rid the lands of violent unrest
We proudly embark upon our quest
Late on, we halt by a village pond
A young victim I see, torn face, hair of
blonde
Snarling she leaps, then stops, sucks her
lip.
I panic and cleave her from neck through
to hip.

A look of apology etched on her face
She falls to the ground with harrowing
grace.
My wounds are bloody, but generally
slight.
The men relish the humour from the tale
of my fight.
A disfigured girl, I took my chances
They tease and boast of my ill-thought
romances.

Terrors awake as the moon climbs high,
Hot throbbing pain, potions inadequately
try
To dull the senses and heal open wounds,
But my life force ebbs and the men talk of
tombs.

"One more day," I plead and beg of the
night.
Pain lay upon me; it makes me contrite.
A golden dawn breaks, a brand-new
tomorrow.
I should be glad not lost in sorrow.

I reflect on my wound, a burning pain,
And somehow, I just don't feel the same.
My head is so empty, a complete lack of
thought,
"Oh Lord, it's not me!" I've come to nought.

I stumble unsteady, devoid of all hope.
Legs shaking beneath me, off I lope.
My mind reels back, hot pain like a flare
Skewers my reason, but leaves me aware.

I see a young woman, blood warm and
tasty
But my attack's thwarted; I am too hasty.
Falling, I grab and hold to her hand,
Bite down on instinct and so, damn the
land.

Stabbed through the heart and in both of
my thighs,
I bleed away slowly beneath angry skies.
Returning pain taunts me; my legs are
now gone.
But my foremost concern is, I have no-
one.

Over days, flesh decays, alone I lie,
But despite all my prayers, I do not die.
Each night descends with monsters
anew,
"No more death, no more nights," I beg of
you.

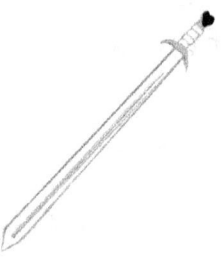

"Knight Horror" is an extract from "Fyrebane's Apprentice"
To Be Released: Summer 2021

What Possessed You?

"But I feel fine..."

"I don't care, you need an *Exorcism!*"

"I'm just the same as everyone my age. Okay, we do things you might consider risqué, you're old, but it's cool."

"**GOOD** Demons don't trail flesh through my clean sulphur! When your father comes home, that human had better be gone."

Never force Karma! Limerick

A man tried to force his destiny
He'd hunt fur and get rich instantly
When he joined outlawed culls
Seals ate his sail and his sculls
Now he's floating, adrift, all at sea.

Spiritual Appraisal

"You say he doesn't threaten you, scare you or worry you?"

"Nope! He just sits quietly for a moment, then shouts...

'Woo Hoo!'

Then he fades; quite nice really."

"It's worse than I thought. She's haunted by a charismatic apathetic orgasmic apparition."

Author!

I am the anathema of heroes and more;
From future cowboys to wizards of yore.
I know what you're planning,
Please join the queue.
When my keyboard cools down,
I'll get around to you.

Bipolar Chance

It wasn't poison, but then
 It wasn't nectar and when
  I swallowed the potion, the bile
  Burned in my throat a short while.

  Then, my headache went
  And the argument
  Was lost to me anyway.

 The bipolar witch
 with the rapid eye twitch
 was actually **GOOD** today.

Drowned Pedant

The boundless sterile ocean stretched before them, limited only by the fiery red sky.

"Water, Water everywhere and we're about to sink!"

"Ha! Wrong! It's, '...not a drop to drink'."

The psychic turned her mournful face toward the only other survivor.

"Give it a moment."

Pet Project

"It's just so ugly!"

"Look, God says he's had enough and can we finish the beasts."

"But look at its thick armoured skin."

"He calls it the Pachyderm series."

"What's that on its face?"

"A huge prehensile nose, it also has a great memory."

"I suppose it's better than the blind one with the horn."

Heavenly Taste

The aesthetic is pleasing, the taste is divine,

Accompanied by a well-chosen wine.

The devilish sauce is hot and abrasive

The recipe please...

and don't be evasive.

"It's just beans on toast, on an Archangel's

wing,

It brings angel delight to everything."

Deadly Fashion.

Writing my latest sci-fi 'Work in Progress',
sat in a café, considering whether to drop the
contagion angle when I realise...

...no-one knows my name and I'm wearing a
red top.

Mired

"Doom! Doom! I say."

"What the...?"

"120 unemployed in the first month. £2 million in orders... lost. By next week this factory will close. The shareholders will shut you down. You'll be ruined! Call yourself a CEO. Which moron died and left you in charge?"

"You did, father."

Sci-Fi Pitch

Marketed to the rich and powerful as 'Resurrection',

"A sure-fire way to extend your influence beyond the grave."

The Sims walked among us.

With no need to eat or sleep, our leaders became megalomaniacs, and now they'll pay.

Outlawed by the people, the war has just begun."

Snow Angel

I made an Angel in the snow
It wasn't happy, it let me know.
"It's freezing, it's dark, it doesn't feel right."
And so, I said, "Let there be light!"

I kept the light and removed the heat
The Angel thanked me for my feat,
"What will you do with that fearsome glow?"
And that's why Hell burns, down below.

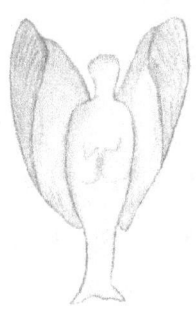

Pummelled by Life

We glide across wavelets, serene
Black waters of the Styx
The oars shipped by centre beam
My whole life amounts to Nix.

The chaos I endured before
I vow I will not miss
It tenderised my immortal core
I'm primed now, for the Abyss.

Odd one out.

If we take it as red

That we all lose our head

As time ticks along a straight line

Then the oddity be

The person you see,

Who dies of old age, while in their right

mind.

Lie Alone

Those whose lies on oath abound,

Dismay the heroes underground.

They fought together, but died alone,

Interred rags and broken bone.

Sedate remains in urns and jars,

Undisturbed by passing cars

Family from our recent past

Their memories fade, their honour's last.

For every misplaced untrue word

Fosters hate for each one heard.

Selfish dreams of those who seek

To sow dissent, with phrase oblique

Who feign remembrance, for just one day,

When deemed their sacrifice will pay,

Bolster their status, add to fame

Investing glory, burning shame.

They ransom your emotions deep,

Betray brave souls and spirits' weep.

Always Be kind to Witches

A witch is a Witch!
Never demon, beast or bitch!
With veracity though predictably unkind.

Be careful what you say
Even in the light of day
You never know when she is stood behind.

She cackled with alacrity
And waved her wand excitedly
Now with full viridity, I hop inside my mind

Monster sculls

Deep red ripples make me nervous as I row
across the loch.
'Neath the waves the monster lurks, a type of
Jabberwock.

Crashing fins, teeth and maw, a terrifying
scene.
I grit my teeth, "Attack or Die!" and wake up
from my dream.

Boat and sculls replace my ship, no more my
armed trireme.
And I notice as I drift, a seagull's eaten my ice
cream.

Careers Interview

"...you might as well say you swim or you walk. Now, come along explain yourself."

"I'm a Farmer. My father was a Farmer and his father before him."

The Officer from Canis Major simply heard the words 'Man of Earth' in his headset.

The Clerk shook his appendage.

The man tutted.

Galactic career agencies were always difficult.

Dangly Thing

A strange periapt passed down from my

gran,

Only for girls, never a man.

It's ugly I don't like it, but it strangely charms

my cat.

Stitched together halves of a mouse and a

bat.

I don't think she was magical, a little mad

maybe.

I wish she hadn't willed this ugly thing to

me.

It's not a rude word.

It was more than a desire. Within the penetralia there was life, and with life came hope.

Outside, beyond the walls, there was nothing but Oblivion, death was only the beginning.

The door became more than a simple portal, beyond was the point of no return.

Fantasy Limerick

A barbarian set everyone's castles alight

To show off his unassailable might

He'd call fighters rude names

Cheat at gambling games;

He'd do anything at all, to start a good fight.

Oh No!

The blood flowed slowly beneath the door. Hesitantly, the carrel was opened and the scene revealed.

It was the seventh defilement within the abbey and the sigil carved upon the cleric's body completed the curse.

Tonight, the demon would rise and the order would burn.

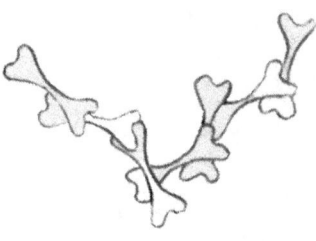

I am True Evil

Ahh! Chaos is the pure way
While other villains seek to slay
And pour on evil every day

I rule the roost with my desire
A murder here and then a fire
Build their hatred ever higher

But then I satisfy a need.
They cease to die, just merely bleed
And thank me as I intercede

Cruel Times

I was a vamp who fed on blood

But loneliness meant that I should

Cut back the bites

Try new delights.

Watch them dancing. A brand-new ploy;

Ingurgitate their heartfelt joy.

No need to cull

Gratuitously full.

But Covid came with all its fears

And now I starve, on salted tears.

Soul Transfer

The plague took them all, the village
destroyed.

We couldn't move on; magic was employed

We begged the Witch, "Help us; we pray!"

"I'll bring them back dear... if you can pay."

Spell cast! The village moved as any other
day,

But dead bodies were awkward and souls
went astray.

A young girl of eight in a body so old,

Fingers stiff she would scream, showing
teeth filled with gold.

Confusion, their Hellish existence a trial.

The mad crone cast again, still in denial.

Gift of the Gods

"Careful with that!"

"Why, what is it?"

"That's all the Orenda we've got... for the whole planet."

"What's it for?"

"We pick the best sentient life and infuse them with it, that way the Gods can leave the health and care of the planet to the locals."

"What happens if I drop it?"

"Don't! We'll end up with another Earth."

One Night Stand.

She's winked now... twice
She looks quite nice
A kiss to end the night.

I take her home
And while alone
My nature caught alight.

The lion's roar that signals power
My sensuous snake within her bower
That turns my dreams to luscious dread.
Demonic needs rise in my head.
The wild rapacious goat uncaged
Chimera sex drive, now engaged.

Dad's philosophy:

I knew my life would taste of blood
My father told me so:
"This world is Hell it reeks of pain. There's
nothing down below."

"But strive and make your life the best. Love
and share and care.
It's the only way to graduate and know the
joy up there."

Cavalry

They stood in silence below the sheer cliff. The men resplendent in their blue and gold, a red pennant upon each lance.

The horses proud, not a sound nor a misstep from the ranks. The discipline was rigid, their prey cornered.

Isolated and trapped, the injured birdman watched as the crows descended and fed.

Divine Magic

Demogorgon, the Elven King
Rules below, o'er everything.
Bestows his gifts for a bargain price
Though not alone, through artifice.
His servants phrase the documents
That add and hide impoverishments
He thinks his gifts bring hope benign
The naïve king of magic divine.
He passed his gift and *Merlin* shone.
Arthur, he chose, to be the one.
Merlin divined what was needed
The magic chose 'HOPE' and *England* was
seeded

Hell

I run down the street, breathless. The pain slices through my chest.

I glance behind, they're still there, suits following, guns in hand. They don't break sweat.

I duck down an alley, they follow close behind. A wall looms ahead, I know where I am. Turning left...

I run down the street, breathless. The pain slices through my chest.

Sword and Sorcery

I've written a book about fantasy.

Where damage is a desirable quality.

Evil wizards have wands,

There's a knight whose oath bonds,

While Dragons spit fire and so do the

blondes.

But as I recall, the worse of them all,

Was a demon possessed, onion seller from

Gaul.

Body warmth.

The coughing stopped in the early hours and the darkness squeezed its frigid air through my bones.

I snuggled down amongst my friends to get cosy. The cadavers stared back, silently accepting the intrusion without complaint.

Soon, I'd be as warm as they.

Conformity

"A brave choice, but change it back to blue and white."

"But...?"

"You know how we do things, leave it like that and they'll hunt you down. You'll get a mock trial; maybe they'll torture you. If you're lucky, banishment or possibly even *crurrk*!" he drew his finger under his neck.

"But I like yellow, Papa Smurf."

Final Escape

Demons break through love's embrace,
To rescue hate and so replace
Thoughts of mercy, pure and kind;
Corruption of the human mind.

And shadows linger like no other
To watch as man reviles his brother.
We wake to death each passing day
While Angel's weep and turn away.

Holiday Memories, Day 1.

70 million years and two and a half thousand miles to see a real dinosaur.

The pod was comfortable, but small for six.

Harry the guide had to shoot the T-rex that ate Marge, the dog groomer, so guess what's on the menu... tastes like chicken.

Holiday Memories, Day 2

Dinosaurs... no fun.

Loads of teeth and scales and a lot of hiding.

Chase back to the pod was exhilarating.

Lars tripped; door won't shut properly 'cos of the teeth marks.

I became concerned when Harry had to kick the engine to get it working.

Holiday Memories Day 3

Ah, well! Breaks over and we're back in our own time.

Cleared customs, handed in the witness reports for the guests we lost.

Harry's twitching less.

Glad to see the timeline is unaffected and Zeppelin's rendition of the Birdy song is still a classic.

Let sleeping Dragons lie.

Dragons know the anagram,

that doth their secret keep.

Towards the last in Finisterre their

elders go to sleep.

But all the dragons know the word obscures

their homely pyre.

Recovering from their daily tasks they often

Rest-In-Fire.

The Last Dance

We danced; it was heaven; when we touched
a flare of love lit up our hearts.
Too soon it ended, but I offered to walk her
home.

We kissed at the gate and I felt a chill.
She invited me in; I hesitated.

"Don't be silly, we're neighbours," she
laughed.

Beside her grave my beaten body lay.

Gamer's Life

I flew my space-ship off to Mars,

Built my home amongst the stars.

Raised my mount a stallion wild,

Destroyed two demons, both reviled.

But now the boss has spoken aloud,

"Retire or be disavowed"

I stomp to bed with scowling mask

Convinced I need another task.

Game over man…!

"G'night"

Succubus

He's drawn to her eyes and lips so red

I feel a shiver of pure dread.

He smiles at her and she winks back

I notice now, her teeth are black.

He sees her arch her nubile shape

The hairs stand up upon my nape

She beckons him, an audience granted.

I mourn the loss, my friend enchanted.

Fairy Infirmity: Limerick

Sprites, Elves and pixies live happily

Skulking about 'neath the willow tree.

But Werewolves and Vamps

Prefer castles with ramps

For their elder, infirm high-born royalty

When I died.

Death was quite a shock!

People staring,

Past Sins bearing

Judge's ruling, in the dock.

No explanation

About damnation

Or elevation high.

My destination?

The next waystation!

"Walk this way, don't cry."

I thought it would be easier to die.

Alchemist's Scent

In the home of the Alchemist

Within the jars the gases twist.

This one's clear the smell is sweet.

This is rancid like rotten meat.

This one's acrid it burns my nose.

This burrows deep exposing my woes.

This one's bright it lights the room.

A new effect from each, per fume.

Adventurer

"This silly map in the front, did you do that?"

I smiled at my disparaging 'fan'.

My Main Character was 'thin', my plot untenable and my map was 'silly'.

"Must be all of ten minutes work in that!" she derided.

"My atlas was the real trick." I boasted. "Creating the fauna, flora, rules of an alien nature, religion and politics."

She rolled her eyes.

"Then, of course, there was creating you lot."

Original Sin

There's only ever been **ONE** deadly Sin.

Stating "There's Seven!" was falling right
in.

Demons set traps by naming the seed,

But if it's a sin, it's always down to Greed.

Wrath, Sloth, and Gluttony are things we
see,

While Pride, Lust and Envy writhe
internally.

But Pride and Envy can spur competition

And a little touch of Sloth aids
recuperation.

Though each rots the soul deep down
inside.

It's Greed that dictates, how far we slide.

Magical Motivation

Rituals for safety and spells to seek revenge.

Wizards killed the demons,

While Sorcerers built Stonehenge.

Magic felt unreal to me, hardly heaven sent.

But now I've found some chicken feet,

...there are disasters to prevent.

Archaeology 2150

It says "Home on the Range... where the... buffalo roam." The archaeologist marvelled at the discovery.

"What's a buffalo?" the intern asked.

"A huge wild animal, hunted by the early tribes before the Climate War, for its meat, and hide," he explained.

"Sorry professor... what's an animal?"

The Greatest Power

"The greatest power is Evil; it feeds those around us and destroys all that is Good."

"No, the greatest power is Love, it creates peace from war and eliminates Evil, providing bliss for all."

"Sadly, both are strong, but seek dominium to bind us. The greatest is Harmony. It is the only choice that sees all things endure."

Acolyte

"Notice how he hangs his head and wrings his hands, apologising for his very existence."

The hooded masters mocked the initiate.

"Shush," whispered the cowled figure beside the judge.

"How can you hope to serve our cause?" The booming voice assailed the newcomer.

The cowed figure straightened, "I bring nothing, my Lord, but my zeal.... and my thermonuclear device"

Fairy Tale Dance

With pluck and aplomb
We entered the room
Our hearts as light as our feet
With lust and romance
We started to dance
Entranced by the partners we'd meet.

A Fairy, an Elf
A Cyclops by himself
The rhythm shook the floor
But when witches arrived
Casting moves improvised
I ran out through the open french door.

Murder?

The body was torn, the choice offal ripped apart. Blood stained the grass.

"Body found by a runner, sir. A local man, no relation."
The face was cut, the eyes gone.

"Do you think it's murder?"
I looked at the silent mass of black feathers staring down.

"I suspect a murder..."

Inevitable insult

"So, the hero strides forward to save the day. You seek to topple my Empire and destroy me. Presumptuous, yet inevitable."

"First of all, I'm no hero. Second, I've a dodgy knee, striding anywhere is out of the question. Thirdly, I'm lost. I slept past my bus stop... What Empire? I thought this was the bus station."

Devoured

(The act of writing my recent book)

From within the shell of my broken mind

I watched it devour my soul.

My life was forfeit, I understood now,

Existence, no longer my goal.

The ancient abyss stared through my heart

I shuddered; my world icy cold.

All belief torn away; my faith ripped apart

As my final chapter was told.

The hero survived, I'm not sure how

The planet destroyed below

Unhinged, I'm adrift, what to do now,

In my heart a new tale starts to glow.

The Cavernous Opening

The ship attacked, all guns blazing, but the agility of the scout was superb.

"Almost there," she screamed her exultation.

A beam took out the thrusters and the scout wallowed, awaiting its doom.

The cavernous opening was black and empty.

"No more coins, love, sorry."

Use 'Fumblejack'
               ...in a sentence, correctly.

It has been decided that since the incident with the archbishop, no frozen asparagus is to be handled by the duty Fumblejack on a Wednesday.

(Now you try.)

Hope.

...but hope is useless, insubstantial, like smoke in the wind. Trust to your heart, your will, your determination.

You, must make it happen!

But if you're really knackered, then hope is a good second choice.

What does magic mean to you?

The Power to awe
To fit the absence
To complete the win
And salve the conscience

Thank you.

Elemental euphoria embroiled with such

emeritus entities.

Emphatic enjoyment ensued.

My thanks to all who got this far.

Don't be shy, all feedback welcome.

@CHart_author

chris@mollyandcorry.com

**Love it or hate it
Chuckle or cringe
Send me your comment,
Your praise or your whinge.**

Other Books by Chris Hart

Gravity Divine

Fyrebane's Apprentice

Molly and Corry Series

Boot up
Satellite Sleuths
Smash 'n' Grab
Digital D-Day